Disney

PIRATES of the CARIBBEAN

ON STRANGER TIDES

Movie Storybook

ADAPTED BY
JAMES PONTI

BASED ON THE SCREENPLAY BY
TED ELLIOTT & TERRY ROSSIO

SUGGESTED BY THE NOVEL BY
TIM POWERS

BASED ON CHARACTERS CREATED BY
TED ELLIOTT & TERRY ROSSIO AND STUART BEATTIE AND JAY WOLPERT

BASED ON
WALT DISNEY'S PIRATES OF THE CARIBBEAN

PRODUCED BY
JERRY BRUCKHEIMER

DIRECTED BY
ROB MARSHALL

Disney PRESS   NEW YORK

All rights reserved. Published by Disney Press, an imprint of Disney Book Group. No part of this book may be reproduced or transmitted in any form or by any means, electronic or mechanical, including photocopying, recording, or by any information storage and retrieval system, without written permission from the publisher. For information address Disney Press, 114 Fifth Avenue, New York, New York 10011-5690.

Printed in the United States of America
First Edition
1 3 5 7 9 10 8 6 4 2
V381-8386-5-11046

ISBN 978-1-4231-3943-0

For more Disney Press fun, visit www.disneybooks.com
www.Disney.com/Pirates

TO PASS THE TIME WHILE AT SEA,
sailors often sang songs called chanties, which told stories of
life on the ocean and celebrated legendary captains. A favorite
chanty was about a notorious pirate who was the scourge of the
British Navy.

★ ★ ★

The Royal Navy did set sail upon the ocean blue
In search of a pirate and his wretched crew—
Looking for a skull and bones on a flag of black,
These royal sailors hoping to capture Captain Jack.

They searched the ocean far and wide for the Black Pearl,
They rode along with every tide and every eddy swirl,
Through island breeze and salty seas and even channels narrow,
They were not pleased that they could not seize the wily

Captain Sparrow.

This song was just one of many that poked fun at the desperate attempts of the king's men to capture the elusive Captain Jack Sparrow. They had come close many times, first at Port Royal and later at Tortuga. But somehow Jack always managed to get away. Always that was, until today.

News spread that Sparrow had been captured not on the ocean but in London. Considering his years of piracy on the high seas tormenting the Royal Navy, the arrest of Jack Sparrow was big news.

On the day of his trial, the courtroom filled with people who booed and hissed as he was led into the room with a black hood over his head.

They'd all heard of Jack's exploits as a pirate of the Caribbean. But apparently none of them had ever seen him—because the prisoner beneath the hood wasn't Jack!

"I told you the name is Gibbs," the man pleaded when the jailer removed the hood. "Joshamee Gibbs!"

No one believed him. After all, it would be just like a pirate to lie.

Joshamee Gibbs was a pirate, but not one worthy of a hanging. He was once first mate on the *Black Pearl* and had come to London looking for Jack. Somehow he'd been mistaken for his friend and arrested.

Just then, the Honorable Justice Smith walked into the courtroom wearing a robe and powdered wig. However, there was something odd about him. He didn't act prim and proper like a judge. Instead, he kind of swaggered—like a pirate. He held a handkerchief in front of his face so that no one could get a good look at him. When he moved it out of the way for just a moment, Gibbs could not believe his eyes.

Justice Smith was actually Captain Jack Sparrow. Somehow the pirate had taken the place of the judge and was now impersonating him.

Jack banged his gavel to call the court to order. Once everyone quieted down, he skipped the trial altogether and ordered the guards to take Gibbs directly to the prison at the Tower of London. The crowd began to riot, and many of them threw shoes, fruit, and whatever else they could find at Jack. He threw some of it back at them before rushing out of the courtroom.

Outside, Gibbs was loaded into the back of a horse-drawn paddy wagon. For a man used to life on the sea, prison was a cruel fate. A few moments later Jack got into the back with Gibbs, who figured that Jack had also been captured.

"Crikey!" he said upon seeing his friend. "Now we're both off to prison."

Jack flashed his gold-toothed smile. This was all part of his plan to rescue Gibbs. "Not to worry, I've paid off the driver," he assured him. "In ten minutes we should be outside of

Londontown. Then it's just a matter of finding a ship."

Joshamee smiled. He couldn't count how many times Jack had saved his life.

Sparrow asked him how his troubles had started, and Gibbs said that he'd come to London because he'd heard Jack was there assembling a crew.

"Am not," Jack said, wondering how such a rumor had gotten started.

"But that's what I heard," Joshamee replied. "Jack Sparrow's in London with a ship and looking for a crew. Fact is, you're signing men tonight at a pub called the Captain's Daughter."

"Am not," Jack said again in frustration. "Truth is Jack Sparrow arrived in town just this morning to rescue Joshamee Gibbs from one appointment with the gallows."

Gibbs nodded and thanked his friend.

Jack didn't like the fact that someone was pretending to be him. He was already in enough trouble for the things he actually did. He didn't need an imposter getting him blamed for others that he didn't.

"What about you?" Gibbs asked Jack. "Last I heard you were bent on finding the Fountain of Youth. Any luck?"

For hundreds of years, explorers and sailors had searched for the Fountain. According to legend, anyone who drank from the freshwater spring would regain their youth and energy. Whoever controlled the Fountain could live forever.

Jack gave a wry smile as he pulled out a map and showed it to Gibbs. "I'll taste those waters," Jack replied. "Mark my words."

Joshamee slapped his friend on the shoulder. "There's the Jack I know." He stared wide-eyed at the map, which showed the Fountain's location and had diagrams of the ritual that would unleash the waters' magical powers. This ritual required the tear of a mermaid. Gibbs gulped at the thought of encountering a mermaid.

Just then the wagon came to a sudden stop.

"Short trip," Jack said as he took the map back from Gibbs and slipped it into his coat pocket.

When Jack and Gibbs climbed out of the paddy wagon, they were stunned to discover that they were now in the courtyard of St. James's Palace, the home of King George. The driver had double-crossed Jack.

The royal guards surrounded them with their rifles drawn and were ready to fire on command. Jack and Gibbs were trapped.

The captain of the guard smashed Jack in the head with the stock of his gun. Jack crumpled into Gibbs's arms before falling to the ground. Another guard shoved Gibbs back into the paddy wagon and slammed the door shut.

Jack was taken into an ornate dining room inside the palace. He was chained to a chair right in front of a long table filled with delicious-looking food. Jack was starving and desperately wanted some of the food. But no matter how hard he tried to get free, the chains made it impossible.

Moments later, a line of royal guards marched into the room. They were followed by the king's advisors. Finally, King George himself entered. Before even saying a word, George plopped down at the table and started devouring the feast all by himself.

"I've heard of you," the king said as he munched on a thick piece of meat.

Jack was proud that his reputation had reached the King of England.

"And you know who I am," George continued.

"The face seems familiar," Jack answered slyly.

The king's prime minister bellowed, "You are in the presence of George Augustus, Duke of Brunswick-Lunenburg, Arch-treasurer and Prince-elector of the Holy Roman Empire, King of Great Britain and Ireland." The man gave Jack a sideways look before adding, "And of you."

Jack smiled. "Doesn't ring a bell."

George gnawed a chunk off a giant turkey leg. "I am informed that you have come to London to procure a crew for your ship."

"Not true," Jack said, wondering again how this story had started.

"**I**'m quite certain that's what my minister told me," the king replied midchew. "'Jack Sparrow has come to London to procure a crew.'"

"It may be true that that's what you were told," Jack answered. "But it's nonetheless false that I have come to London to procure a crew."

"Ah," George said as he turned to his guards. "You've brought me the wrong wastrel. Find Jack Sparrow and dispose of this imposter."

Jack didn't want to be disposed of.

"Wait! I am Jack Sparrow. The one and only," he said, holding his hands up to signal the guards to stop.

Finally, convinced he had the right man, King George had Jack's chains removed and explained his problem. "I have a report that the Spanish have located the Fountain of Youth." He started to angrily tear a loaf of bread into small chunks. "I will not have some Spanish monarch gain eternal life!"

King George knew that Jack had long searched for the Fountain and had even heard that Sparrow had a map to it. If the stories were true and the Spanish had one as well, the king did not have time to waste. He needed Jack's help.

"**Y**ou do know the way to the Fountain?" George demanded.

"Absolutely," Jack answered with a wry smile.

"And you could lead an expedition?"

"You'll be providing a crew and a ship?" Jack said, smiling.

"And a captain," added the king.

Jack's smile disappeared. He wanted to be the captain.

"We believe we have found just the man for the job," the minister said.

He motioned to a guard, who opened the door. Jack sat upright and heard footsteps approaching. Actually, it was a footstep followed by a long scrape. Then another footstep followed by another long scrape. This pattern continued until the mysterious captain emerged from the darkness, his tall frame filling the doorway.

The man walked with a wooden peg leg and was dressed like a naval officer. But while the peg leg and clothes were new, the face was the same as it had always been. The king's captain was none other than Jack's archenemy, Hector Barbossa.

Jack immediately confronted Barbossa about the ship he'd taken from him. "What became of the *Pearl*?"

Barbossa explained that the *Black Pearl* had sunk, yet he had survived. "Lost her," Barbossa said. "Lost the *Pearl*. Lost my leg. I be genuine contrite on both counts."

Jack arched an eyebrow. "Lost?"

"I defended her mightily, but she be sunk nonetheless," Barbossa said.

Jack pointed out that it was the duty of a captain to go down with his ship, and that if the *Pearl* had sunk Barbossa should be dead.

The two of them argued, and Jack used this argument to create confusion in the room. When it did, he made a daring escape. The guards were blocking the door, but Captain Jack Sparrow didn't need a door to escape.

He jumped on the table and used that to leap onto a giant chandelier. He swung on the chandelier over the heads of the surprised guards and jumped out a window, escaping along the roof. He even managed to eat a cream puff on his way!

"Round one to Jack Sparrow," Barbossa said as he watched the guards chase after him. He knew they wouldn't catch him. But he was also certain that he and Jack would cross paths again. They always did.

Jack headed straight for the pub called the Captain's Daughter. That's where Joshamee Gibbs said the phony Jack Sparrow was supposed to be signing up his crew. Jack figured that if he made a surprise visit he might be able to catch the imposter red-handed. He also might be able to get his hands on the imposter's ship.

The Captain's Daughter was loud and dirty and had a foul stench about it. It was filled with cutthroats and scallywags who all seemed on the verge of breaking into fights. In other words, Jack felt right at home.

In the rear of the pub, he saw a line of sailors waiting by a door. The door was guarded by Scrum, a beefy sailor who sat on a stool and strummed a mandolin to pass the time. Jack asked an old man what was going on.

"Those folks," he said, pointing toward the storeroom, "have a ship and are looking for able hands." Jack had found what he was looking for.

Jack came up from behind Scrum and put a knife against the mandolin player's Adam's apple. "I hear you be recruiting a crew," Jack whispered in his ear.

"Aye," answered Scrum nervously. "That is, Jack Sparrow be putting together a modest venture."

"Don't you know who I am?" How was it possible that this sailor thought someone else was Jack Sparrow?

Just then the door opened and a young pirate burst in with a smile on his face. He'd just signed on with the crew. The sailors in line congratulated him and slapped him on the back.

Jack stepped into the room and could not believe what he found. Standing in front of him was none other than. . . Jack Sparrow! Or at least someone who looked exactly like Jack Sparrow, with the same outfit, the same dreadlocked hair, and the same swagger.

"You've stolen me," the real Jack said angrily, drawing his sword. "And I'm here to take myself back."

The phony Sparrow did the same, and within seconds Jack was virtually having a sword fight with himself. The two "Jacks" matched each other thrust for thrust and lunge for lunge. Even their footwork was identical!

"Stop that!" an annoyed Jack implored.

The sounds of their clashing swords filled the back room as they climbed up ramps and over support beams. Through it all, the imposter fought just like Jack.

"Only one person alive knows that move," Jack exclaimed as his alter ego perfectly mimicked one of his most difficult maneuvers.

Suddenly, a smile came over Jack's face as he leaned forward and kissed the imposter. "Hello, Angelica," he said. He removed the imposter's hat and fake beard to reveal that phony Jack was actually a beautiful woman.

"Hello, Jack," she replied. "Are you impressed?"

"I am touched at this most sincerest form of flattery," he said. "But why?"

Angelica laughed. "You were the only pirate I thought I could pass for."

Jack thought for a moment. "That is not a compliment," he decided.

Years earlier, Angelica had fallen for Jack, and in return he had been less than honest with her. Jack had turned her into a pirate, but because Jack was always on the lookout for new treasure and new adventure, they parted ways.

Together again, they instantly began to argue. Jack started quarreling about her pretending to be him, while she wanted to fight about their relationship years before. Their argument was interrupted by the king's guards, who had arrived at the pub looking for Jack.

"Friends of yours?" Angelica asked, exasperated.

Sparrow smiled. "I may have unintentionally slighted some king or another."

"You have not changed," she said with frustration. They may have been mad at each other, but neither one wanted to be captured by the king's men.

"May I suggest an alliance," Angelica offered as she slashed a rope, unleashing a stack of barrels that came crashing onto the guards as they entered the room.

"This way!" she said as she led Jack through a maze of crates until they reached a trapdoor in the rear of the warehouse. It led to the river Thames, which flowed dangerously far below them.

"Desperate disease . . ." she said.

"Requires dangerous remedy," he completed.

They splashed down in the river and swam until they were out of view of the guards. As they climbed up the bank, Jack was relieved to have escaped again. Just then, he felt a sharp pain in his neck. He reached up and was surprised to pluck out a voodoo dart. His world started spinning, and the last thing he saw was a large man hulking over him. The man's eyes were completely dead and white.

Just before Jack fell unconscious he uttered one final pronouncement: "Zombie."

The poison from the dart kept Jack unconscious for days. When it finally wore off, he woke up at sea on the deck of a pirate ship. He had no idea where he was or how he got there. A sailor handed him a mop and told him to start cleaning. It was Scrum, the same sailor who'd been playing the mandolin at the pub.

"Um, there's been a mistake," Jack said to Scrum. "I'm not supposed to be here."

Scrum cackled. "Many a man's woken up at sea with no idea why and no memory of the night before."

"No, you see, I am CAPTAIN Jack Sparrow," he said. "The original."

"Scrum," the sailor answered. "The pleasure's all mine. Keep moving."

Scrum pointed out that there were some pretty scary officers on the ship and that they had to keep working. Jack started mopping as he tried to figure out what had happened. "Where am I?" Jack asked.

"I be right honored to welcome you aboard our eminently infamous vessel," Scrum told him. "The *Queen Anne's Revenge*."

Jack knew the name well. The *Queen Anne's Revenge* was one of the largest, most notorious pirate ships to ever sail the seas. And he knew the captain's name, too.

"Blackbeard," he said aloud to himself, more than a little worried.

Blackbeard had a murderous reputation. And what Jack saw over the next few hours only confirmed it. The officers of the *Queen Anne's Revenge* were ruthless. They whipped anybody who even looked at them the wrong way. They were terrifying. Jack noticed one who was particularly gruesome. His lips and one eye were sewn shut.

"That fellow seems odd," Jack mentioned when he passed. "French is my guess."

"He's been zombie-fied," Scrum explained. "Blackbeard's doing. All of the officers are that way. Keeps them compliant."

Jack nodded. "And perpetually ill-tempered."

This was not good news. Jack was stuck on Blackbeard's zombie-filled pirate ship—and on his way to the Fountain of Youth. Plus, the Spanish and English navies were also on their way to the Fountain. Things got worse when Jack heard Scrum mention that the ship's first mate was a woman.

That's when he realized that this had to be Angelica's ship. She had tricked him! He searched the ship until he found her on the gun deck. He jumped out to surprise her and held a sharp cargo hook to her throat.

"You are a ruthless, soulless, cross-grained cur," Jack said.

Angelica smiled. "I told you I had a ship."

"No," Jack corrected. "Blackbeard has a ship. Upon which I am now imprisoned."

Angelica pushed the hook away and looked Jack in the eyes. She wanted to find the Fountain just as much as he did. "We can pull this off, Jack. The Fountain of Youth. Like you always wanted."

Jack gave her a dubious look and motioned in the direction of the captain's quarters. "Edward Teach," he said, using Blackbeard's real name. "The pirate all pirates fear. Resurrector of the dead in his spare time."

"He'll listen to me," Angelica said.

"He listens to no one," scoffed Jack.

"Perhaps he would listen to his own daughter?" Angelica inquired.

"Ah, but you're not his daughter" Jack expertly pointed out. Angelica then flashed him a devilish smile.

Jack was stunned as Angelica laid out her devious plan. She had actually convinced Blackbeard that she was his long-lost daughter. And, now that they were reunited, he trusted whatever she told him.

Jack had to admit it was a clever plan. But he didn't quite see a role in it for him. "Then it's the Fountain of Youth for him, or him and you," he said. "Not you and I."

"No, Jack, that's the best part. He'll be dead."

For years, people had been trying to kill Blackbeard only to wind up dead themselves. Jack had no desire to join them. "You'll be handling that part yourself?" Jack asked.

"There is a prophecy—the man with no eyes," Angelica said, referring to the zombie who had shot Jack with the dart in London. "He is known as *eleri ipin,* which means 'witness of fate.' What he says comes true, and he has seen Blackbeard's death," she replied.

"**Y**ou believe that?" Jack wondered.

"He believes it," she explained of Blackbeard. "That's why he needs the Fountain, Jack. He can feel the cold breath of death down his neck."

Angelica told him that since Blackbeard thought he was dying, he desperately needed to reach the Fountain of Youth before the zombie's prophecy came true. And, since Jack was the only one on board who had seen a map to the Fountain, he'd be the navigator.

Jack thought about the plan but was still troubled. He knew that Blackbeard couldn't be trusted. And he was pretty sure he couldn't really trust Angelica either.

Jack realized that in order to get what he wanted he needed to take over the ship. He knew that the crew was miserable and terrified of the zombies, and he decided that this offered the perfect chance to convince them to mutiny. He spread word among them to meet in a storage cabin.

It was night and the only light in the room was the dim flicker of a candle placed on a wooden crate. The meeting place had an eerie quality, which Jack hoped would make the crew more likely to join his scheme.

"The topic is mutiny," Jack said just above a whisper. "Mutiny most foul."

Like him, the other crew members were not happy that they'd been lied to. They'd thought they were signing on to a crew led by Jack Sparrow, not Blackbeard. And they'd had no idea they'd be tormented by zombie officers.

"Blackbeard," Jack continued. "What are his habits?"

Oddly, none seemed to know. It turned out that none of the crew had ever actually seen Blackbeard on the deck.

"**A**ny of you sailed with him before?" Jack asked.

The pirates all looked hopefully from one to another, but no one said a word.

Jack couldn't believe it. "No one's sailed with him. No one's seen him," Jack said with a laugh. "Good news, gentlemen. This is not Blackbird's ship. This is not the *Queen Anne's Revenge*."

Jack was convinced that it was all a trick by Angelica. Just as she had pretended to be him in London and pretended to be Blackbeard's daughter, she had also pretended that this was Blackbeard's ship.

Now the crew was really angry. And that's when Jack realized that none of them knew where the expedition was headed. When he told them they were searching for the Fountain of Youth, they were terrified. There were countless stories of sailors who'd died horrible deaths trying to reach the Fountain. They thought it was cursed.

"It'll mean death for certain!" cried one sailor.

"Unless," Jack said, seizing the perfect moment, "we take the ship."

On his orders, the pirates charged through the door and took to the moonlit decks, attacking the zombie officers. The battle was raging, and the mutineers were winning.

"Fight to the bitter end!" Jack screamed to rally them.

Soon after, all of the officers had been subdued, with most of them lashed to the mast.

Jack's plan had worked, and he would now take over as captain. He'd still lead them to the Fountain of Youth, but he'd be in charge.

"The ship is ours!" he announced triumphantly.

To his surprise, this was not greeted by cheers from the men. Instead, they stared past him with frightened looks on their faces. Jack slowly turned around and saw what they saw. Silhouetted against the moon was the looming figure of Edward Teach, better known as the notorious Blackbeard.

Blackbeard looked across the deck of his ship and tried to control his rage. His officers were lashed to the masts, and his crew had done the lashing.

"Excuse me, gentlemen," he boomed. "I be placed in a bewilderment. I be Edward Teach, Blackbeard, and I be in the captain's quarters. Aye? And that makes ME the captain."

The crew shuddered with fear, and Jack quickly tried to devise some explanation as Blackbeard walked ominously among them, slowly drawing his sword.

"What of this on deck?" Blackbeard continued. "Sailors abandoned their posts without orders! Men taking the ship for their own selves? What be that, first mate?"

"Mutiny!" answered Angelica.

"Aye," Blackbeard said as he continued to walk among them. "And what be the fate of mutineers?" he sneered. At this point he reached Jack and looked him right in the eye before saying, "Mutineers HANG!"

Suddenly, the ship's ropes appeared to come to life. They wrapped around the mutineers and lifted them high into the air. It was as if Blackbeard were controlling the ropes by mere thought.

Without missing a beat, Jack, who was now hanging upside down, spoke against the crew he had so skillfully convinced to mutiny.

"Captain, sir, I am here to report a mutiny," he offered. "I can name fingers and point names!"

"No need, Mr. Sparrow!" he bellowed. "They are sheep. You, the shepherd."

Jack was released from the ropes and fell to the deck with a THUMP. It seemed as though Blackbeard might run him through right there, but Angelica came to Jack's rescue.

"Father," she reminded him, "he has been . . . to the place where we are going."

Jack happily added, "Have I told you, sir, what a lovely daughter you have?"

"Mercy, Father," Angelica pleaded.

Blackbeard thought about this for a moment. "If I don't kill a man every now and then, they forget who I am," he said with an evil laugh. But he still needed Jack in order to find the Fountain of Youth.

Blackbeard had two of his most terrifying zombies bring Sparrow back to his cabin. Jack worried that he might have run out of ways to escape.

"I've no interest in the Fountain," Jack said, lying. "But what about the mighty Blackbeard?" he asked.

"Every soul has an appointment with death. In my case I happen to know the exact time," Blackbeard replied with a smile. "I must reach the Fountain. It be foolish to battle fate, but I am pleased to cheat it."

Just then Angelica came into the cabin.

"Oh, good. He's still alive," she said seeing Jack healthy and breathing. "You will lead us to the Fountain, yes?"

Jack squirmed for a moment. He didn't want to join forces with someone as treacherous as Blackbeard. Plus, there were already two other expeditions racing to the Fountain.

Then Blackbeard leaned in close and made the decision simpler for him.

"Put another way," the evil pirate said. "If I don't make it there in time . . . neither will you."

Jack nodded. He would help. He had no other choice. He'd join forces with Blackbeard and try to beat the others to the Fountain. Once he got there, then he could try to figure out how to get rid of Blackbeard.

He flashed his gold-toothed smile and said, "I'll have a look-
see at those charts, straightaway."

It wasn't enough just to reach the Fountain of Youth. To
unleash the magic of its waters, they had to perform the ritual,
and for that they would need a mermaid's tear.

Jack used the charts to help guide them to beautiful
Whitecap Bay. The crystal blue water lapped up against a rocky
shore where an old abandoned lighthouse stood. But beneath the
surface, Whitecap Bay was infested with the foulest, most evil
creatures to swim the oceans of the world.

Whitecap Bay was home to the mermaids.

Catching a mermaid was not easy, and Blackbeard's plan required the entire crew. Jack was part of a group sent to a nearby lighthouse. They needed to get the light working again to attract the mermaids to the surface.

As they climbed the steps to the top, Jack told a young pirate all about what they were facing. "You ever see a mermaid?" he asked him. "Nasty as hungry sharks. With weapons. And they're all women."

"Beautiful women?" asked the young man dreamily.

Jack shook his head in frustration. "Did you miss the part about the sharks?"

That was the power that mermaids held over sailors. They were so beautiful that the sailors forgot about how dangerous they were.

To lure the mermaids to the surface, a longboat was sent out with a crew of young pirates, including Scrum.

"Sing!" a zombie officer told him. "They like to hear singing."

Scrum began to sing a chantey he knew well. "My heart is pierced by Cupid, I disdain all glittering gold. There is nothing can console me, but my jolly sailor bold!"

Just then a mermaid surfaced right next to Scrum's boat.

"You're beautiful," he said, mesmerized.

The mermaid smiled. "Are you my 'jolly sailor bold'?"

"Aye," he said with a smile. "That I be!"

Suddenly a group of mermaids surrounded the boat, each one smiling at one of the pirates. Despite the warnings the men had received, these creatures were very beautiful and were irresistible to the pirates.

"I'll have it said that Scrum had himself a kiss from a mermaid," he said proudly.

Scrum leaned close to her. But just as their lips were about to touch, the mermaid made a terrifying shriek. The kiss turned into a bite as she pulled Scrum under the water.

Before the other pirates could react, the rest of the mermaids did the same. Within seconds Whitecap Bay was filled with the sounds of shrieking mermaids and screaming pirates.

In keeping with the plan, other pirates started dropping explosives into the water. Then Blackbeard ordered men with nets to wade into the water from the beach. "Out upon it," he commanded as he carried a burning torch along the waterline. "We need but a single one!"

Jack shook his head as he watched the battle unfold. Wherever he looked, it seemed as though the mermaids were winning. He cared about his shipmates and wanted to help them, so he decided to make a weapon out of the lighthouse.

Its flame was slowly fed by a stream of whale oil which it burned to stay lit. There was a giant tank of the oil, and Jack wondered what would happen if more of it reached the flame.

He took out his sword and smashed open the tank so that the oil sprayed in every direction. Then he jumped out the window to safety. Once the oil reached the flame, the entire top of the lighthouse exploded into a giant fireball that rocked the whole beach and blasted across the surface of the bay.

"Did everyone see that?" Jack asked. "Because I'm not doing that again!"

The mermaids screamed in horror and let go of their victims. That was just the chance the pirates needed to get free. They rushed toward the safety of the beach.

And there, on the beach among the debris, was a mermaid, injured but still alive. She was trapped in a tide pool and unable to swim to freedom. A missionary sailor named Philip rushed to her aid, but first a zombie threw a net over her!

Blackbeard placed the mermaid in a giant aquarium that he had constructed so that she could stay alive in the water but couldn't swim away. Now, with the mermaid in tow, the crew began to march through the jungle toward the Fountain.

But there were problems. The Spanish and British navies—and Hector Barbossa—were also searching for the Fountain, so the race was on. And even more terrifying was the fact that Jack was with Blackbeard. Once the nefarious pirate no longer needed him, Jack was certain Blackbeard would want him killed. But Jack had been in dire situations before and always seemed to survive. And now as he looked at a chance for eternal life, he started making up a sea chantey of his own, right on the spot.

There was a pirate, Captain Jack,
who was so brave and bold,

Stuck on a voyage to the Fountain
that left him rather cold!

He faced the Spanish and the
British and even the evil Blackbeard,

Yes, Captain Jack Sparrow was
the one pirate that everyone else
feared!

★ ★ ★

A sly smile spread across Jack's lips as he recited his made-up chantey. Captain Jack knew that this would indeed be a most memorable adventure, even if it did find him trekking through a dangerous jungle and setting sail on stranger tides. . . .